MW01043157

Text copyright © 2025 by Marilyn Sadler

Cover art and interior illustrations copyright © 2025 by Steph Laberis

All rights reserved. Published in the United States by Random House Children's Books,
a division of Penguin Random House LLC, 1745 Broadway, New York, NY 10019.

Random House and the colophon are registered trademarks of Penguin Random House LLC.

Visit us on the Web!
rhcbooks.com

Educators and librarians, for a variety of teaching tools, visit us at RHTeachersLibrarians.com

Library of Congress Cataloging-in-Publication Data is available upon request.

ISBN 978-0-593-81033-0 (trade) — ISBN 978-0-593-81034-7 (library binding) —
ISBN 978-0-593-81035-4 (ebook)

Book design by Michelle H. Kim

MANUFACTURED IN CHINA
10 9 8 7 6 5 4 3 2 1
First Edition

Random House Children's Books supports the First Amendment and celebrates the right to read.

Penguin Random House LLC supports copyright. Copyright fuels creativity, encourages diverse voices, promotes free
speech, and creates a vibrant culture. Thank you for buying an authorized edition of this book and for complying with
copyright laws by not reproducing, scanning, or distributing any part in any form without permission. You are supporting
writers and allowing Penguin Random House to publish books for every reader.

It's Not Easy Being a LEPRECHAUN

written by Marilyn Sadler ✳ illustrated by Steph Laberis

Random House New York

Connor O'Connor was not a happy **LEPRECHAUN**. He was much too small. His ears were far too big. And he looked like a lawn ornament. But worst of all, no one wanted to be his **FRIEND**. All they wanted was his gold!

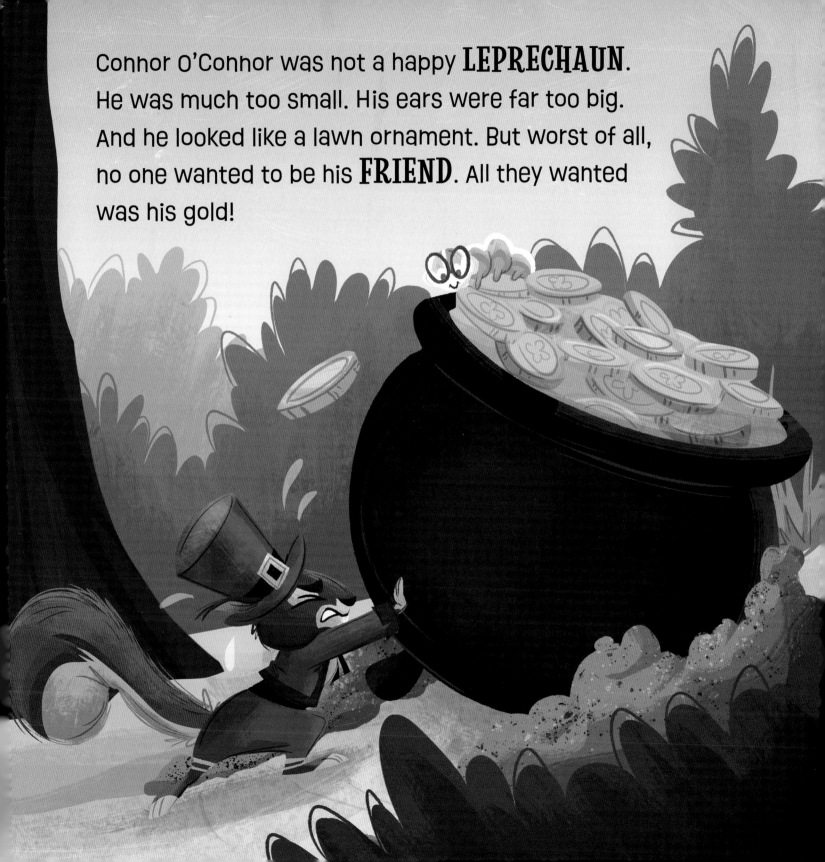

"I **DO NOT** want to be a leprechaun!" he said.
So he hung up his hat. He hid his pot of gold.

And he set off on his merry way.

"Top of the morning!" he said to a **FAIRY** he met in the forest. She was smaller than he was. But she could fly!

If I could fly, I wouldn't care that I was small, he thought.

So he cast a magic spell and turned himself into a **FAIRY**!

Connor fluttered up above the trees. But when he looked down, he remembered he was **SCARED OF HEIGHTS!**

Connor **DID NOT** want to be a fairy!

So he set back off on his merry way.

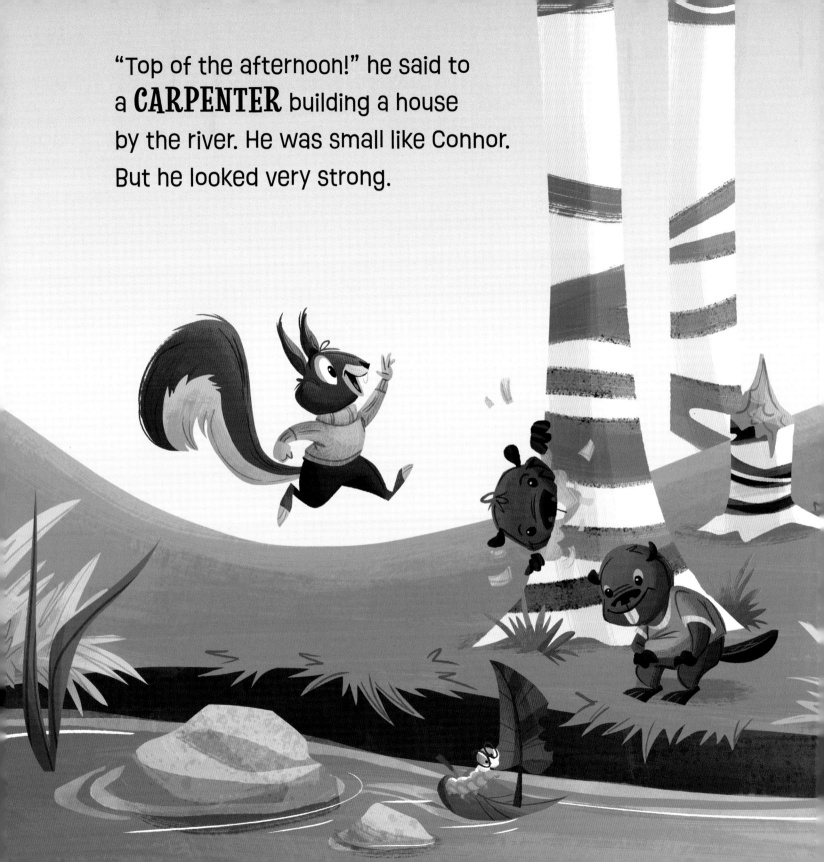

"Top of the afternoon!" he said to a **CARPENTER** building a house by the river. He was small like Connor. But he looked very strong.

If I were a carpenter, at least I wouldn't look like a lawn ornament! Connor thought.

So he cast a magic spell and turned himself into a **CARPENTER**!

But building a home by the river was **EXHAUSTING**!

Connor **DID NOT** want to be a carpenter!
So he set back off on his merry way.

"Top of the evening to you!" he said to a **KING** he met along the road.

If I were a king, he thought, *I'd live in a castle, and no one could steal my gold!*

So he cast a magic spell and turned himself into a **KING**!

But living in a big castle was **VERY LONELY**!

Connor **DID NOT** want to be a king!
He was about to go on his merry way . . .

. . . when he spotted a princess by herself in the garden.
She looked as lonely as Connor felt.
"Are you okay?" he asked.

"No," said the princess. "I am very sad. I live in a castle, and I have many beautiful things. But the one thing I WANT—and do not have—is a **FRIEND**!

Will YOU be my friend?"

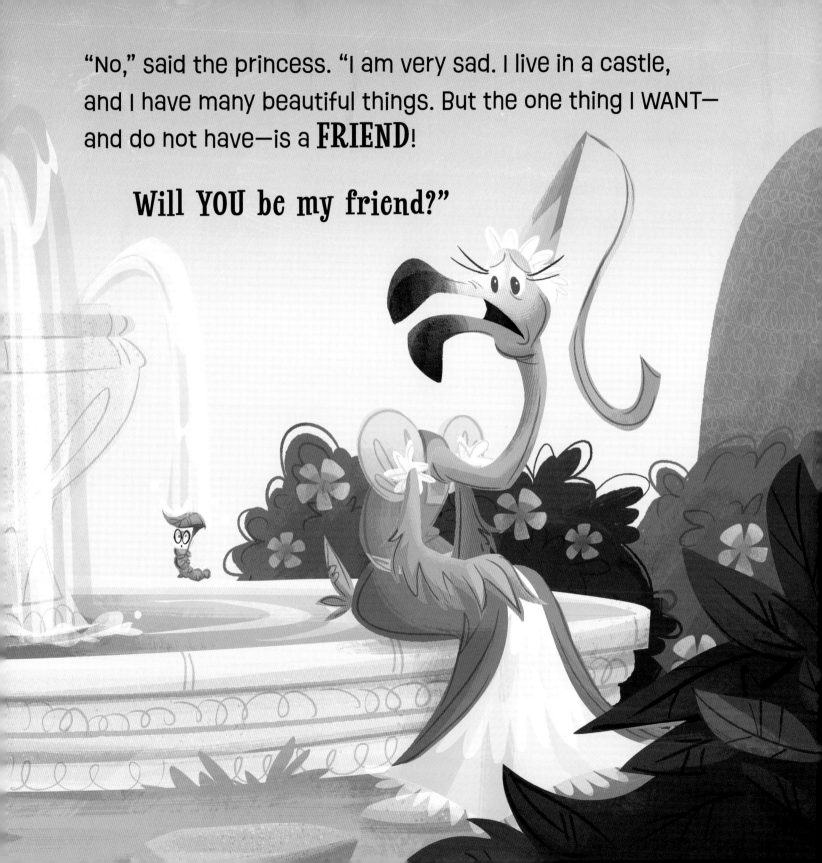

Connor was so surprised his crown almost fell off his head! "I would **LOVE** to be your friend," said Connor. "But I don't know how to turn myself **INTO** a friend!"

"It's the easiest thing you will ever do!" said the princess. "You just have to **BE YOURSELF.**"

So Connor cast a magic spell and turned himself back into a **LEPRECHAUN**!

He was short. His ears were big.
He looked like a lawn ornament.
And everyone wanted his gold.

But now he was also a **FRIEND**!

Connor and the princess found many ways
to spend their time together . . .

. . . and many ways to spend his gold!

"It's not easy being a **LEPRECHAUN**," said Connor.
"But there's NO ONE ELSE I'd rather be!"

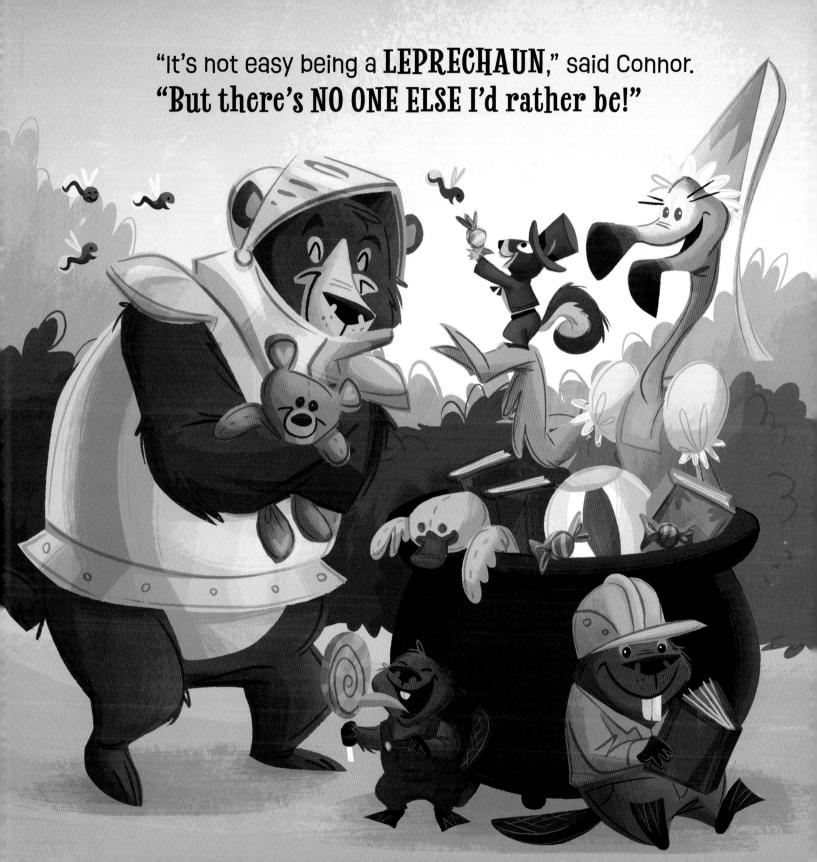